# Malorie Blackman
## Illustrated by
# Colin Mier

CORGI PUPS

www.kidsatrandomhouse.co.uk

For Neil and Lizzie,
with love

SPACE RACE
A CORGI PUPS BOOK : 978 0 552 54542 6

First publication in Great Britain

PRINTING HISTORY
Corgi Pups edition published 1997

9 10

Copyright © Oneta Malorie Blackman, 1997
Illustration copyright © Colin Mier, 1997

The right of Malorie Blackman to be identified as the
author of this work has been asserted in accordance with
the Copyright, Designs and Patents Act 1988

Set in Bembo Schoolbook

The Random House Group Limited supports The Forest Stewardship
Council (FSC), the leading international forest certification organisation.
All our titles that are printed on Greenpeace approved FSC certified paper
carry the FSC logo. Our paper procurement policy can be found at:
www.rbooks.co.uk/environment.

Corgi Books are published by Random House Children's Books,
61–63 Uxbridge Road, London W5 5SA,
A Random House Group Company

Addresses for companies within The Random House Group Limited
can be found at: www.randomhouse.co.uk/offices.htm

THE RANDOM HOUSE GROUP Limited Reg. No. 954009
www.**kids**at**randomhouse**.co.uk

A CIP catalogue record for this book is available from the British Library.

Printed and bound in Great Britain by
Cox & Wyman Ltd, Reading, Berkshire.

Made and printed in Great Britain by
Cox & Wyman Ltd, Reading, Berkshire.

# CONTENTS

Chapter One
## The Challenge                    7

Chapter Two
## The Plan                         21

Chapter Three
## The Race Begins                  32

Chapter Four
## Beaten!                          42

Chapter Five
## The Secret Weapon                51

Series Reading Consultant: Prue Goodwin
Reading and Language Information Centre,
University of Reading

# OUR SOLAR SYSTEM

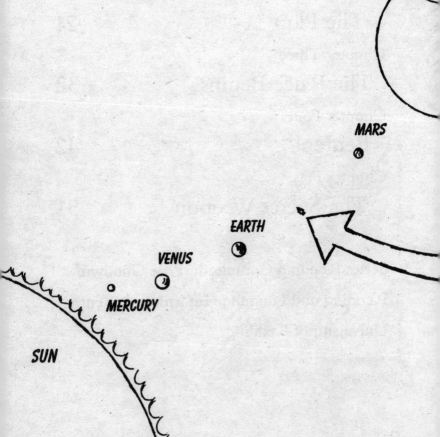

MARS

EARTH

VENUS

MERCURY

SUN

PLUTO

NEPTUNE

URANUS

SATURN

JUPITER

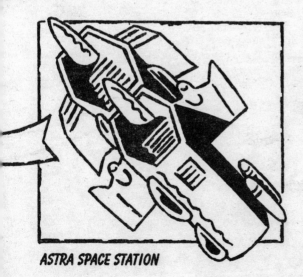
ASTRA SPACE STATION

# CHAPTER ONE
## The Challenge

Lizzie loved living on the Astra
Space Station. All her friends on
Earth were so jealous when her
family moved out there. Lizzie
had soon made lots of new
friends and it was great fun.
There was just one problem. Jake!
All he did was brag and show off.

Today he was at it again, boasting about his brand new, super duper, fat-ace, deluxe spaceship. "It's got the latest computer so all I have to do is tell it where I want to go and when I want to get there and the computer does the rest. And my new ship's fast because it runs on diamond fuel.

It's one of the first ships anywhere on this space station to run on diamond fuel," said Jake.

Huh! If he was any more pleased with himself he'd pop like a balloon, Lizzie thought to herself.

"I bet I've got the best spaceship in the whole school," Jake continued. He looked around the classroom. "It's a lot better than any of your ships, that's for sure."

Lizzie had had enough. "Jake, I bet my ship could beat yours any day."

The words were out of Lizzie's mouth before she could stop them. Jake burst out laughing – and he wasn't the only one. Some others in the class also creased up. Everyone else just looked at Lizzie as if she was seriously nuts!

"You must be joking!" Jake scoffed. "Your ship couldn't beat mine if I gave you one year's head start!"

"You don't have to give me a head start. My ship can beat yours any day of the week," said Lizzie, stubbornly.

"OK then. Let's have a race.
Out to Pluto and back. The first
one back to this classroom wins,"
said Jake.

Lizzie swallowed hard. Oops!

"Now you've done it!"
whispered Lizzie's best friend,
Sarah.

And Sarah was right! It was one thing for Lizzie to say her ship could beat Jake's, but it was quite another to prove it. Lizzie's spaceship was old and it only ran on emerald fuel. Jake's ship ran on diamond fuel so it travelled a lot faster than hers ever could.

"I. . . I. . ."

"You're going to back out, aren't you?" Jake said smugly.

"No, I'm not going to back out. OK, you're on," said Lizzie. "We'll have our race this weekend."

"Oh no we won't. Let's have our race now," said Jake.

"But it's lunch-time," Lizzie protested. "We can't race to Pluto and still be back here for our first lesson after lunch."

"I can!" Jake smiled. "I can race to Pluto and back in about fifteen minutes!"

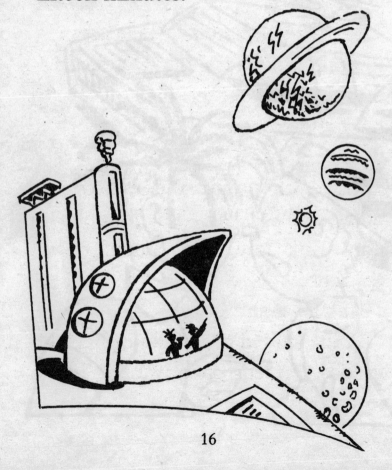

Lizzie's heart sank. She knew
it would take her at least an hour
and a half to get to Pluto and
back. How could she get out of
this?

"Jake, I hope Lizzie does beat
you," said Naren. "Then maybe
you won't show off so much."

"Yeah!"

"That's right!"

Lizzie smiled gratefully at her
friends. At least they wanted her
to win.

"She doesn't stand a chance and you all know it," Jake said with his usual smirk on his face.

"Jake, I'll race you, but let's have our race tomorrow – early. How about at seven o'clock in the morning?" said Lizzie. "I need to tune up my ship's engine first."

"That's fine by me," Jake shrugged. "And you can tune up your ship all you like – you'll still never beat me."

"We'll see about that," said Lizzie.

And she was determined that there was no way Jake was going

to win the race. He needed to be taught a lesson. The only trouble was – he was right. Lizzie couldn't beat him. Not unless she came up with a plan first.

# CHAPTER TWO
## The Plan

Later that day after school, Lizzie and her friends gathered in the pizzeria. The space station had lots of different places to eat but they all liked pizzas the best. Lizzie gazed out of the window at the Earth below and sighed. What had she let herself in for now?

"So what're you going to do?"
Naren asked.

"I haven't a clue!" Lizzie
sighed again and leaned her
head on her cupped hand. She
stared down at her dinner plate.
She hadn't touched her Andorian
beetle pizza and it was usually
her favourite. She just didn't
seem to have much of an
appetite.

"Don't you want your dinner?"
Darla asked.

Lizzie shook her head.
Immediately, many different hands
reached into her plate for her
beetle pizza. Naren won!

He chewed on the pizza with
obvious relish, enjoying it all the
more for the look of
disappointment on his friends'
faces.

"If you haven't got a plan, why on earth did you want to race at seven o'clock tomorrow morning?" asked Darla.

"I was hoping Jake would say it was too early!" Lizzie replied.

"No chance!  Jake would race you at three o'clock in the morning if it gave him a chance to show off!" sniffed Naren.

Just then,
Sarah came
into the
pizzeria. She
took a quick
look around
before making
for Lizzie's
table.

"D'you
know what I
just heard?"
Sarah asked
furiously.

Everyone
shook their
heads.

"No?
What?"

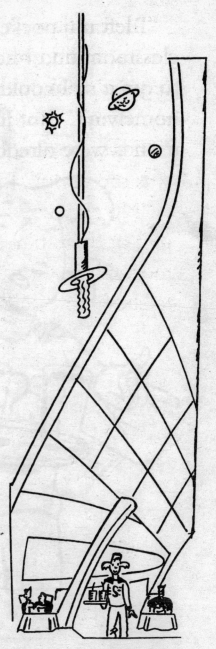

"I left my pocket-PC in the classroom and I had to go back to get it so I could do my homework. But Jake and his friends were already there.

Lizzie, Jake's going to make sure that you don't win. He's going to sabotage your ship's engine tonight so there's no chance of your beating him."

"What a trog!" Darla exploded.

"You said it." Lizzie nodded vigorously. "He doesn't have to fix my ship. His ship could beat mine fair and square."

"Jake doesn't know the meaning of the word 'fair'," Sarah sniffed.

"We've got to teach him a lesson. We've *got* to! Come on, Lizzie – *think*!" Lizzie told herself sternly.

She had to come up with a plan, but what? And then it hit her – like an asteroid shower!

"I've got it! I've got it! I know
how I can win this race and
teach Jake a lesson once and for
all," Lizzie told her friends.

They looked at each other.

"We're all ears!" said Sarah.

"Good! Because I can't do this
without your help," said Lizzie.

"I'm going to need each and every one of you."

"We're with you, Lizzie," said Naren.

And they all gathered closer to hear Lizzie's plan.

# CHAPTER THREE
## The Race Begins

The following morning, at seven o'clock precisely, Lizzie and Jake entered docking-bay three. Both of their ships were there, waiting for take-off.

"I'm surprised you bothered to turn up," Jake told Lizzie.

"I'm going to win this race," smiled Lizzie.

"You've got space fever!" Jake replied.

"We'll see!" Lizzie climbed into

her spaceship without another word. Once they were both cleared for take-off, the countdown began.

Five... four... three... two... one! And they were off!

Jake roared ahead at once. He veered towards Lizzie's ship, forcing her to drop back or risk being smashed into. Jake watched, his hands relaxed behind his head as Lizzie's ship fell further and further behind.

By the
time he
had
passed
Mars,
Lizzie's
ship
was no
more
than a
small blip on
his rear

viewscreen. Jake slowed down
his own ship. He certainly didn't
have to hurry. Lizzie would
never catch him now. He'd seen
to that.

Jake spoke to his computer.
"Computer, connect me through
to Lizzie's ship."

Immediately Lizzie's face appeared on the space communicator.

"If you want to give up now, you'd save us both a lot of time and energy and you'd save yourself a lot of humiliation," Jake told her.

Lizzie frowned at him. "Jake, why on earth would I give up when I'm ahead of you?"

"What're you talking about?" said Jake.

"Look out of your front viewscreen," said Lizzie. "I'm approaching Jupiter now. You should be able to see me ahead of you."

"You can't be ahead." Jake was stunned. "You were thousands of kilometres *behind* me."

"Not any more. I spent all of yesterday evening fine-tuning my ship and what's more I've got a secret weapon. You'll never catch me," grinned Lizzie.

Jake looked. And sure enough,
up ahead in the distance was
Lizzie's ship.

"What's your secret weapon?
How did you pass me?" Jake was
furious.

"Temper! Temper!" Lizzie
teased. "If you'll admit defeat
now and say my ship is better

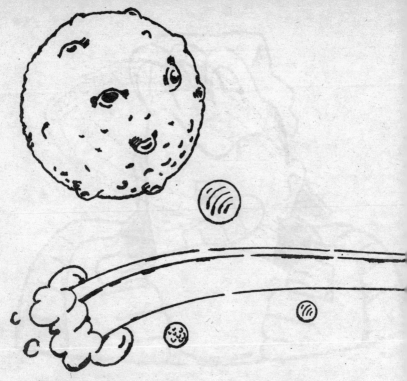

than yours then we don't have to
go any further."

"No way!" said Jake.
"Computer, set course for Pluto
at the maximum speed."

Jake's ship lurched forward and
started to race towards Jupiter.
In less than five minutes, Jake
passed Lizzie's ship. He still

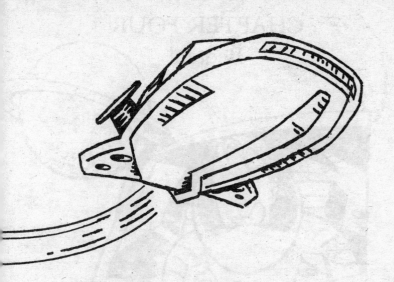

couldn't understand how Lizzie
had passed him but it wouldn't
happen again.

The next stop was Saturn and
after that, Lizzie wouldn't see
him for space dust!

# CHAPTER FOUR
## Beaten!

Jake waited until he passed Saturn before slowing down again. Beaming like a light beacon, he reconnected with Lizzie's ship.

"I don't know how you got ahead of me just now but it doesn't matter – I'm winning again," said Jake.

"I don't think so," Lizzie shook her head. "I've almost reached Neptune so I'm in the lead."

And sure enough, when Jake checked his scanner, Lizzie's ship was indeed ahead of him. Jake just couldn't understand it.

"Computer, go at the maximum possible speed," ordered Jake. "I'm not going to lose this race – I'm *not*!"

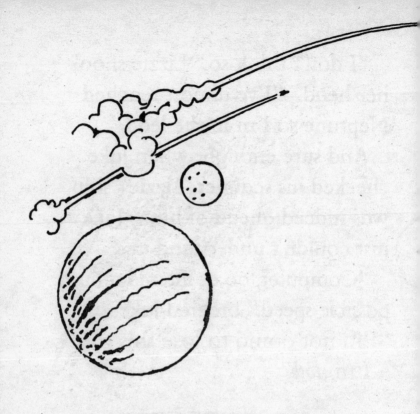

Jake's ship raced past Uranus, towards Neptune. He soon passed Lizzie's ship and headed on towards Pluto. Jake wasn't going to take any chances this time. He wasn't going to slow down until he got back to the space station. No way was

Lizzie going to pass him again.

Jake zipped round Pluto and started making his way back to the Astra space station. He had no idea how Lizzie managed to keep passing him. What was this secret weapon she had told him about? How could any secret

weapon be better than diamond
fuel? Jake scanned the area
again as he neared Neptune on
his return journey. His space
communicator beeped at him.
Moments later Lizzie's face
appeared.

"Come on, Jake. I thought
you'd be able to keep up with me

at least," Lizzie teased.

"What d'you mean?" said Jake.

"I'm coming up to the rings of
Saturn," Lizzie told him. "You're
going to have to do better than
this!"

"How are you doing it?" Jake
asked, bewildered. "How d'you
keep managing to pass me?
I don't even see you until you're
ahead of me."

"That's thanks to my secret weapon. Besides, space is a big place. I don't have to take exactly the same route as you," Lizzie told him.

"But. . ."

FIVE MINUTES AND FORTY-FOUR SECONDS

"See you back at the space station," Lizzie smiled.

"Computer, maximum speed back home," Jake commanded.

"We have been travelling at maximum speed for the last five minutes and forty-four seconds," the computer replied.

Jake sped past Saturn, raced past Jupiter, zoomed past Mars and screeched to a halt back in

docking-bay three on the space station. But it didn't make any difference. By the time he landed, Lizzie was already there, waiting for him. He had been beaten.

# CHAPTER FIVE
## The Secret Weapon

"I want to see this secret weapon,"
Jake demanded.

"D'you admit that I beat you?"
Lizzie asked.

"Yes . . ." Jake said in a tiny
voice.

"I can't hear you."

"YES!" Jake shouted.  "Now can
I see your secret weapon?"

"I don't think so," Lizzie said,

considering carefully.

"Oh but . . . but I'm bursting to know how you managed to beat me," Jake protested.

"If you tell everyone that I beat you, I'll think about it," Lizzie grinned.

Later on that day Lizzie and her
friends, Naren and Sarah and
Darla, all sat down for lunch.
Lizzie looked out of the view-
window and smiled at all the
stars around them.  She loved
living on the Astra space station

– there was always something
new and exciting going on.  And
today was a particularly good
day!  Jake had been beaten!

"Has Jake guessed how we did it yet?" asked Naren.

Lizzie shook her head. "I feel a bit guilty about the way we beat him. After all, we did cheat."

"No, we didn't.  We just used our imaginations – that's all!" laughed Sarah.

"Besides, he was the one who tried to fix the race," Darla pointed out.

"Anyway, you were all brilliant!" said Lizzie.  "I couldn't have done it without you."

Just then Jake appeared, with an expression on his face that none of them had ever seen before. For once, he wasn't smirking.

"Listen everyone!" Jake shouted out. The school dining-hall went very quiet. "This morning Lizzie and I had a race out to Pluto and back and Lizzie beat me. I lost!"

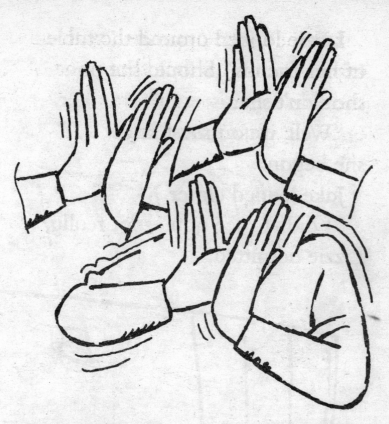

Everyone started clapping! The whole school knew about Jake's boasting, and this was the first time he'd admitted he wasn't perfect! Jake sat down at Lizzie's table. "Now Lizzie, please, please tell me how you did it."

Lizzie looked around the table at her friends. Should she or shouldn't she?

"Well, if you must know . . ." she began.

Jake leaned closer.

"I didn't race you – not really," Lizzie admitted.

"What d'you mean?" frowned
Jake.

"I mean, I got as far as Mars
and turned back," said Lizzie.

"But I saw your ship. First you
were ahead of me at Jupiter and
then I had to overtake you again

at Neptune," said Jake. "And on the way back, you were ahead of me again at Saturn."

"No, I wasn't." Lizzie smiled. "You passed *Sarah's* ship at Jupiter and you passed *Naren's* ship at

Neptune. And on the way back,
you passed *Darla's* ship at Saturn.
One good thing about all of us
having old ships is that they all
look the same. I just came back
here and pretended it was me all
the time."

"So . . . so it wasn't you . . ."
Jake was amazed.

"Nope! My friends were my secret weapon," said Lizzie.

Jake leapt to his feet. "But that's not fair. I'm going to tell everyone . . ."

"How you fixed my engine so there was no way I could beat you?" Lizzie asked. "How you couldn't even race against me fair and square without cheating?"

Jake stared at her.

"How did you find out about that?"

"A little comet told me!" Lizzie replied. "And the next time you have a race, don't cheat! You might find you actually win!"

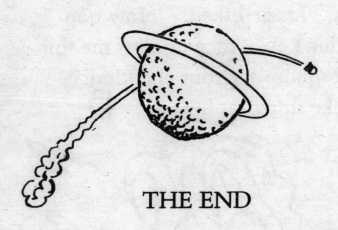

THE END